Mohammed Said Hjiouij (born April 1, 1982) is a Moroccan Novelist. His novel "By Night in Tangier" won the Inaugural Ismail Fahd Ismail Prize (2019). His second novel, "The Riddle of Edmond Amran El Maleh," has been shortlisted for "The Ghassan Kanafani Prize for Arabic Fiction (2022)", and the Hebrew translation is coming soon.

"Kafka in Tangier" has been translated into Kurmanji and excerpts into Hebrew and Italian.

Phoebe Bay Carter is a translator from Arabic and Spanish and a PhD student in Comparative Literature at Harvard University. Her translations have appeared in ArabLit Quarterly, InTranslation, Action Books blog, and elsewhere.

Kafka in Tangier

(A novel translated from Arabic)

Mohammed Said Hjiouij

AGORA Publishing

Tangier, Morocco

AGORA Publishing
Tangier, Morocco
www.kafkaintangier.com

Publisher's Note: This is a work of fiction. Names, characters, places, and incidents are a product of the author's imagination. Locales and public names are sometimes used for atmospheric purposes. Any resemblance to actual people, living or dead, or to businesses, companies, events, institutions, or locales is completely coincidental.

.

Kafka in Tangier/ Mohammed Said Hjiouij. -- 1st ed. 28 February 2023
Dépôt Légal (BNRM): 2023MO0324

ISBN 978-9920-570-28-2

Kafka in Tangier

Translated by:
Phoebe Bay Carter

Goodbye, stranger. Your stay was brief, but wonderful. May you find the paradise you were searching for. Goodbye, stranger. Your visit was a dance of shadows. A drop of dew before sunrise. A tune we heard for a moment from the brush. Then we should our heads and said we'd imagined it. Goodbye, stranger. Yet, everything comes to an end.

.

– AHMED KHALID TAWFIK

CHAPTER 1

The Hero with a Thousand Faces

He read Kafka's *Metamorphosis* before bed. When he woke up the next morning after a night of disturbing dreams, he found himself transformed into a monster in his bed. No, not a large insect like Gregor Samsa. More like a putrid and distorted version of himself. Even so, he knew that his fate would be no different from that of young Samsa: he would die in three months, no more and no less, just before his twenty-seventh birthday.

Good. Now that I've caught your attention, let's go back to the beginning and take things one step at a time.

You ask who I am? Oh, the curiosity of the limited human mind, which cannot hope to grasp me in my enormity! Suffice to say that I have gone by many names throughout human history, among them the Blind Bard, Shakespeare, the Storyteller… Perhaps Scheherezade is the most famous. And now you ask, where are these events taking place? Ah, how limitless the curiosity of your human minds! Really now, is that so important? Fine. Let the setting be Tangier. But not, of course, the city of Tangier that you know. This is another one, which merely resembles it. A Tangier parallel to the one you consider real. But, mind you, being parallel doesn't mean it is made up. Let us agree from the outset that the binary of reality and fiction depends entirely on where you're looking from.

Now, can I get back to the tale? Good.

It began in a sewer. He was running, looking over his shoulder every other step, fleeing from an enormous insect that looked to him, under the dim light, like a cockroach the size of a dinosaur. He was dreaming, of course. I know you are smart enough to realize this, and also to realize that this dream was a predictable result of the story, or novel, that he read before bed.

Before returning home the day before his metamorphosis (this was a Sunday), he had followed his feet that afternoon to Malabatta Beach, which he had not visited in the past five years. He was impressed by the new corniche and the wide plaza, which the municipality had designed in imitation of the Hassan Mosque Plaza in Rabat. But after a few steps, he found himself face to face with an open sewer belching the city's waste directly onto the beach. He saw to his left children swimming gleefully there where the wastewater mixed with the ocean. To his right was a bridge covering a section of the drainage ditch, with cars whizzing over it at such a speed that made it impossible for a pedestrian to cross. He peered down at the sewer, contemplating the water heavy with human waste. Raising his eyes, he saw a man contemplating him from across the ditch. He looked out of place, standing there dressed in black from head to toe. Shiny black shoes and a fancy black suit. Unkempt hair, bulging eyes, and large ears perked to receive the world's buried secrets. All black except for his near-translucent skin, and a small red notebook in his left hand. His eyes were bright with intelligence, but also with a lurking sadness that threatened to take over his entire face. There was something familiar about the face. Very familiar. Maybe he was famous. Surely he had seen a picture of this face not long ago.

He turned away from the man and pulled an envelope out of his pocket. On its corner was a green insignia of a snake swallowing its tail accompanied by the words *Medical and Reproductive Testing Laboratory*. He stared at it for a long time, until his eyes began to water. He pursed his lips. Furrowed his brow. Then let all his features fall slack. He sighed, finally letting the anguish settle onto the blank slate of his face. The envelope slipped from his grasp, and he watched as the breeze tossed it about for a moment, as though rocking a feather to sleep, before laying it to rest on the water's surface. He watched as it floated, drifting with the current until it soaked up the wastewater and was dragged under by excrement.

That bridge, with its concrete pillars sunk into the waste water, was the setting of the dream. The underbelly of the bridge, to be precise.

The further he went into the sewer, the weaker the light became, while the putrid stench grew stronger. It filled his mouth as he gulped down air, trying to get oxygen to his lungs.

He tripped and fell. He went under the thick sludgy water. He got up quickly, spitting and wiping the city's shit from his face. He set off running again at a speed not typically seen in dreams. But, like someone who's cast the evil eye upon himself, he felt a sharp stab of pain in his right leg and fell once more. The insect descended upon him. Its jaws gaped like a T-Rex's as they came closer and closer to his neck.

His heart raced, pounding like a war drum under the arch of the bridge. He realized that until then it had been completely silent. He had not even heard the sound of the water splashing under his own feet. But now he heard his heartbeat like a drum signaling war between two tribes. He wanted to lift his hand out of the water to push away the insect, which had begun to look to him like a great, black dog. It looked like — no, it *was* the hound of the Baskervilles. But, somewhere between his brain and his hand, the nerve signals lost their way. He wanted to scream, an act of desperation when there was nothing else left to do, but his tongue stuck to the back of his throat. He was choking. A shudder wracked his body and a warm stream of liquid ran between his thighs. He opened his eyes.

The first thing he was aware of upon waking was the septic stench that had hitched a ride on his nose from dream to reality. He would soon realize that, in fact, the opposite was the case. The fetid smell had traveled from reality into his dream; or, rather, it was the very smell that was responsible for creating the whole dream just as he was beginning to wake up.

The second thing he became aware of was a numbness spreading across his right side. A numbness punctuated by tingling. It was not unlike pins and needles, but ten times stronger. The strange thing was, he was lying on his left side. Shouldn't he, he thought, have pins and needles on the side he was lying on, not the side up in the air, free from the weight of his own body?

The third thing he became aware of was the warm liquid between his thighs and dripping down his legs. Yes, you know quite well what that means.

But he couldn't believe it. He figured he must still be dreaming. He blinked several times, but nothing changed. The same noxious stench, the same tingling along his right side, and still the same damp below him. So. It wasn't a dream. He cast his gaze around the room. It was indeed his bedroom, of that there was no doubt. His wife asleep on the other side of the bed, their daughter's crib nearby; the antique clock his mother had bought before her own marriage told him it was six in the morning. On the wall facing him were three frames of the Arabic calligraphy he had once so loved to paint, back in the days before life had trapped him with its net and broken his back. This was his bedroom, of that there was no doubt at all. And this was no dream he was living now.

Then, just as he tried to roll onto his back, came the moment of truth. The truth that would make him scream a scream that would shake the building from its colonial-style gables to its concrete foundations. A scream that would echo across the large apartment as it bounced from room to room, knocking on each door and hammering at each eardrum, slinking under the chairs and leaping across the sofas, ricocheting off the walls and ceiling and floor. It would be a long time before the furniture absorbed all the despair and anger and grief of that scream.

CHAPTER 2

Utopia

There is no denying that the tale I am telling you, or the novel, as you call it these days, shares a certain resemblance with the story it inspired, the one written by Franz Kafka over a century ago. That said, it is most certainly not an exact copy. But, like that story, I will pause here for a moment to recount a bit of our hero's backstory before returning to the morning of the metamorphosis, what happened after that, and perhaps how it all came about.

Gregor Samsa was a traveling salesman. He was a young bachelor who, after sacrificing himself and his ambition for five years, decided to continue doing so for several more years in order to support his family (a mother, a father, and a little sister) when his father lost his business and began drowning in debt. The lad had no choice but to work a job he did not like to save his family from poverty. The strange thing was, his family had a cook and a maid despite their apparent poverty. I am not adding this to Kafka's narration; he included this detail himself.

As for the hero of our story, he was married, worked as a teacher during the day and – on the days he returned from school not completely exhausted and dispirited – a vegetable seller in the evening.

He had intended to graduate from the Faculty of Letters and Humanities as a renowned literary critic who would make the whole world toss out all the literary theories of old and embrace his own inimitable theory (which he had thus far only outlined). Alas, he was to abandon his dream, or at least defer it, after his first two years as a student at the Faculty and switch to the Teachers' Institute, from which he graduated a year later as a teacher with glum features and slumping shoulders.

He was 21 years old. During his year at the Teachers' Institute, he worked various trades to cover his expenses. The modest scholarship he received from the Institute, along with his mother's savings which she kept hidden from his father, were barely enough to keep the family alive after his father decided one day out of the blue to quit working, spread his prayer rug in the corner of the house, and spend his days begging his Lord's forgiveness for all the years he had spent working as a bartender.

Before I forget: the Sunday before the Monday morning when our hero discovered his metamorphosis, which would be the beginning of his discovery of his true family ties, he went out for a walk. He did not go to the market where he was supposed to earn his extra income working the vegetable cart. It was not that he was tired, or craving a vacation. He had not gone Saturday either, or Friday afternoon. The reason, quite simply, was that on Thursday afternoon, his cart had been taken from him. I will return to this detail later, of course, but first we are going to talk for a moment about the father. About the lord of the household who suddenly discovered that there was a Lord above him and promptly ceased lording over his household and turned instead to worshipping his newfound Lord.

If we left the task of describing the father to his angry son, he would say he was skinny as a pencil, tall as a lamp post, stubborn as a mule, and violent as a landslide. As you can see, as much as this description clarifies the nature of the relationship between the son, who found himself suddenly bearing the full weight of his familial duties like Planet Earth upon his shoulders, and the father, who had changed all at once for reasons entirely unknown to his family and stopped caring for them without a second thought… But of course there was no need for a second thought. Had he not fathered a son and fattened him up so that he would one day grow up to work and support him? That was a son's only role, after all: to grow up and support his parents, then get married, have kids, and feed them one way or another until they grew up to provide for him and have their own children who would, in turn, provide for their parents. Anyhow. As I was saying, as much as this description clarifies the nature of the relationship between son and father, it also clarifies, in its conventionality and dull repetition, the woefully limited literary talents of this son who dreamed of becoming a literary critic. It is indeed quite lucky that he did not achieve this dream, for he would have ended up merely parroting flimsy opinions that would not have allowed literature to develop as I desire. As a result, I myself would not have been able to develop, for I am only able to do so through the developing tastes of readers.

My god, I've begun to ramble like a child who has learned a new word and thus begins to use it in every sentence, whether the occasion calls for it or not. Forgive me my childish whims. Where were we? Ah yes, we were talking about the father.

The father's worst characteristic was without a doubt his stubbornness. You would see that this is quite natural, however, if you knew that he was descended from one of the rural tribes of Al Hoceima's countryside, where they suckle on hard-headedness along with their mother's milk. The curious thing is that for all the pride he took in his pure Berber heritage, untainted by the blood of the desert Bedouins, he also took immense pride in his family title, Al-Sharif (that is, "the honorable one"), passed down through the Prophet's lineage. "Sharif" was his preferred name at the bar, and he refused his quality service to anyone who failed to respect his honorable place among the Prophet's descendants.

The father was skinny. The sort of skinny that comes bundled with a hot set of nerves. He did not smoke and was smart enough not to drink, so he did not blow all his tips at the bar as many of his coworkers did. And so, in a few short years, he became the owner of a spacious apartment downtown, a remnant of the days of Spanish colonialism. It overlooked *Sour el Maagazine* down onto Port Tangier (and on a clear day you could see all the way to the south coast of the Old Continent from the apartment window). But he was a miser. Or, if you want to be precise, not a miser exactly — but he was careful to spend his dirhams in the right place at the right time. The funny thing is, the one time he broke his own rule, he raked in tips like he'd never dreamed of.

That one time took place on the evening of the eleventh of September of the first year after the end of the second millennium.

The bargoers had begun arriving early, fleeing from the strong gusts of wind that had begun blowing in clouds heavy with rain. At some point, a customer rushed in and asked excitedly to change the channel from the music station to Al-Jazeera. Heads turned and eyes fixed on the screen, which was now broadcasting images of the towers as they turned into two chimneys belching flames and smoke before collapsing, as if a giant hand had descended upon them and flattened them to the ground. Once the surprise passed, the cheering commenced and, for the first time in that bar, exaltations of God's greatness rang out from the crowd. Out of the corner of his eye, the father glimpsed two French customers slipping out. He smiled and announced that the next round was on him. The remaining customers applauded. Later, when the bar was full, he offered, in a moment of madness he could not quite explain, another round of drinks on him. Everyone was celebrating. And everyone was analyzing the situation with the experience of those who had drunk international politics along with their mother's milk. Al-Qaeda's name was tossed about, but quickly discarded. Everyone doubted that an Islamic organization like al-Qaeda had the means to pull off an operation of this magnitude, efficacy, and speed. The kamikaze-style execution made many think of the Japanese Red Army. Others thought it was an inside job, aimed at changing some government policy or passing a new law. No one seriously considered the possibility that the operation was linked to a religious group which classified itself as an Islamic jihadist organization.

That evening belonged to celebrations of the decisive blow that had been dealt to America. The arrogant aggressor had long been asking for a little reproof. Later, sadness for the innocent victims would come. On the evenings that followed, the bar would be abuzz with discussion of the attacks. Some would believe that the victims were innocent, while others thought all the infidels were enemies and needed to be killed wherever they were. Others would say that those citizens were responsible for their government's policies and were therefore complicit in all the tragedies that the United States of America had caused around the world. The father did not care about these discussions. He was still reveling in the handsome tips he had raked in that evening. These bellowed arguments will be repeated among the customers five years later, when Saddam Hussein is hanged on the morning of Eid al-Adha, which will fall on the thirtieth of December of that year. This time there will be no tips, because the argument between those who celebrate the execution and those who see Saddam as the hero the Arabs needed will devolve into blows, leaving the whole bar a wreck.

I will not dwell any longer on this digression from the tale at hand. I will only inform you that the father, as a result of his excessive nervousness and late nights at work, would not tolerate any murmur or movement in the house that would disturb his sleep during the day. All too often, the poor son would accidentally make some noise that bothered the father, who would emerge from his bedroom with puffy eyes and an iron-buckled leather belt. This he would crack through the air and swing at his son at will, leading the son to frequently skip school so that his classmates would not see the marks of the belt-whip on his face.

Now, let us return to our hero.

CHAPTER 3

A Small Death

He blinked several times, but nothing changed. The same putrid stench, the same tingling all along his right side, the same damp under him. He checked again to make sure he wasn't dreaming. He must have worn himself out yesterday, he thought, walking further than he had in years, and then slept wrong, causing part of his body to go numb, which affected his bladder in some way, leading him to lose control over it – a reasonable explanation as to why he had wet the bed at his age. And this last involuntary action was behind the smell. Having explained away his strange awakening, he let out a sigh of relief.

He began to shift onto his back, careful not to wake his wife. He was surprised that the smell had not already done so. Unless the smell was not really as bad as he imagined. He allowed himself a smile and continued rearranging himself.

He had been sleeping on his left side all the way on one edge of the bed, while his wife slept all the way on the other, as far from him as possible. When he went to roll onto his back, he did not realize how close he was to the edge, so as soon as his center of gravity bid farewell to the mattress's firm surface, he found himself sprawled on the floor. He screamed.

The bed was not high, and the pain from the fall was not the reason for his scream.

When he fell and the bedsheet slipped off him, he did not find himself underneath.

No, this was not his body.

The first thing to catch his eye was a forest of hair covering his chest. He raised his head a bit higher and saw that the coarse hair covered his whole body. Then he noticed that all the toes besides the big one on each foot had merged into one broad, flat toe. He turned his head to the right, towards the wardrobe, which had a mirror covering one of its doors. It was then that he let out the scream that would shake every corner of the apartment and wake all the sleepers within. What he saw reflected in the mirror was not him at all. The hairy creature looked to him like a monkey. A short monkey. A dwarf monkey. But he was not short. He had always been the tallest among whatever group of humans he found himself in. This could not be possible. Unless it was just a dream.

But it was not a dream. Not even close.

His wife jumped out of bed in a panic. She clutched a hand over her heart and recited several breathless *bismillahs* as she looked around the room. Her heavy eyes landed on him as he stared into the mirror in horror. Her eyes widened and then it was her turn to scream a scream no less forceful and frightful than her husband's. Then she collapsed into a faint. At that moment, their two-year-old daughter, who until that moment had been asleep in the crib by their bed, opened her Mongolian eyes and plump lips and launched into a fit of crying that would prove no easy feat to quell.

In her own room, his mother bolted out of bed in fright. In the hallway, she found her daughter – his sister – emerging from her room, face pale and eyes red. The mother cast a glance toward her husband, who was pressing his forehead into his prayer rug in the corner of the living room, engrossed in a long prayer that began every day at dawn and did not end until he smelled the morning coffee.

With a racing heart, the mother knocked on her son's closed door and, with lungs gasping for air, asked what was going on. There was no answer other than the cries of her granddaughter who had been awoken, in turn, by her mother's scream, which exceeded her tolerance for sudden noises. The sister jiggled the door handle with anxious, unavailing movements, then tried to shove the door open with as much strength as her slender, twenty-one-and-a-quarter-year-old body could muster, pounded on it with both her fists, and finally cried out, sobbing, to her brother and sister-in-law. No reply besides the cries of her niece, who was not accustomed to such a morning racket.

Meanwhile, the son and brother was still entranced by the mirror. He was frozen in front of the image of the monster monkey, which stared back at him from that other world beyond the mirror. Now that he could see his face clearly, he discovered how it, too, had been disfigured. Half of his face was paralyzed. He remembered reading somewhere that this was called Bell's palsy. The right side of his lips hung limply, and the eyelid on that side had gone slack, leaving the eyeball bulging out to reveal the white of the eye, now almost completely obscured by a web of red capillaries.

His nose had grown accustomed to the putrid smell emanating from his body like the sulfur that might perfume a satanic temple, and he had even begun to feel that his outward appearance was the pinnacle of beauty, when suddenly he felt a flood of filth fill his veins. His heart tightened and his eyes began to water. Then his entire body shuddered as the tingling on his numb right side intensified. He felt violated, as though a strange being had invaded his body and took up residence in it. If he believed in jinn, and their ability to possess humans, he would have thought immediately that the weight of filth he now felt within was nothing other than a legion of demons taking hold of his body. But he did not believe any of that. Although, later, he would recall the novel *The Exorcist* and compare these sensations with the effects of little Regan's possession.

Between the child's sobs, he heard the key turning in the lock. He remembered that his father kept a spare copy of all the keys to the house. He looked around in panic and his eyes landed on the bedsheet. He stretched out his hand and pulled it towards him, then crawled to the corner of the room, covering his body with the sheet just as the door swung open.

He saw his father first. The father looked at his son for a few brief moments and a trace of displeasure appeared on his face before he turned his gaze to rest on his daughter-in-law's body, which was visible through her flimsy, lacy nightgown.

He saw his sister push through the door and stare straight at him. He saw the blood drain from her face, leaving it a garish yellow. Then it was her turn to faint.

He heard his mother's scream before he saw her push his father out of the way and bend over her daughter. Once she had checked her daughter's breathing, she raised her head and he saw the shock etching its mark across her prematurely wrinkled face. He saw her get up quickly, holding back tears, and lift his daughter from her crib before fleeing the room. Then he heard her sobs from the hall.

He saw his father ignore his sister and carry his wife from the room.

His sister began to come to. She pushed herself up to sitting. Waves of pain, fear, sadness, pity, and terror washed over her face as she looked at him. Then she started to cry. He wanted to help her up, to console her, he who needed consolation more than anyone, but his father came back in and helped his daughter up and out of the room before locking the door behind him.

His mother managed to calm the child. Silence reigned for a little while, and then he heard his wife's sobs. He imagined her sitting on the sofa, hugging her bare legs, the white of her thighs surrendered to his father's gaze.

He heard his father's voice creeping toward him across the floor, slipping under the bedroom door, passing next to the bed, and climbing his legs to finally enter his ears, drenched in hatred and loathing, carrying four words: "What is this demon?"

He closed his eyes in sorrow, then lifted his head and scanned the room. He noticed that during his fall, he had knocked over the reading lamp, along with a book that had been on the table next to the bed. He remembered how his hand had reached out instinctively when he lost his balance and tried to catch himself on the table that served as his desk. But his hand had landed on the book he had been reading before bed, causing both hand and book to slip. He fell, and the book fell with him onto his face.

His gaze fixed with surprise upon the picture on the cover. Now he remembered where he had seen that face before. The man all covered in black that he had seen by the sewer, who had seemed so familiar yesterday – he looked like Kafka! No, he *was* Franz Kafka. Unless this was all just in his head.

CHAPTER 4

The Dead Zone

He wasn't sure that he actually hated his father. His childhood certainly hadn't been easy. The fact that his father worked nights and slept days gave them little chance to develop a normal relationship. Add to that the father's nerves, and his disproportionately violent responses to what were usually trivial infractions committed by the son, we find that if the son did not in fact hate his father, he most certainly did not love him. No feelings of affection towards his father were to be found in the son's heart. Or if there ever were, they must have leaked out during those cruel days when the son found himself, suddenly and unexpectedly, bearing the whole family on his shoulders. However, let us not forget that this family considers itself a traditional, conservative, Moroccan family from the North. And in these parts, you will always find respect for the father in the heart of his son, even if it is motivated by a sense of duty and nothing more.

In spite of that, or perhaps because of it, he could not quite grasp the hatred in his father's rhetorical question, nor the loathing on his face when he looked in and saw his son's illness. Yes – his illness! He clapped his hands. He had found an appropriate word to describe his condition. He was ill! The filth he felt coursing through him was nothing but an illness. He threw the sheet off and tried to stand up, talking to himself all the while. Every disease has its cure, and surely this illness was no exception. But he did not make it to standing. He was stabbed once more by pins and needles and he collapsed in pain, a moan escaping his drooping lips like a howl – a howl that wracked his body with a shiver of pity for himself and everyone who'd heard him. He guessed that his mother would now cover her face with her hands and cry over his pain. Indeed, he could actually see her on the other side of the wall, exactly as he'd guessed. And he saw his sister get up to rock the baby girl, who had started crying again, and his wife turn her face away from their bedroom door, and his father pick up a glass of water from the table and fling it at the bedroom door. It shattered with a crash that drowned out, for a moment, the sobs of his mother and daughter.

When the glass hit the floor, he felt his heart shatter along with it. He recalled how Gregor Samsa had suffered a similar agony when he came out in the morning and his family saw that he'd become a filthy animal – a dirty, putrid insect. His mother fainted and his father started crying. As for the secretary sent by his manager to find out why he'd been missing work, he jumped with fright and fled the apartment, leaping down the stairs as though pursued by demons and forgetting his walking stick, which the father then used to beat poor Gregor back into his room. He was injured in several places before the door closed on him, and he crumpled to the floor in shock, his wounds oozing blood.

At least he was better off than Gregor, he thought. As a civil servant, his salary would be guaranteed for months while a cure was found for his illness. The only time he had ever relied on his father's help was just before his graduation from the Teachers' Institute, when one of his father's acquaintances had intervened to make sure he was appointed to teach somewhere within Tangier's city limits, unlike the rest of his classmates, whose luck flung them to the mountain regions with its cold villages cut off from the outside world all winter. Now he would have to turn to his father once more, and for the last time, to bribe a doctor to write a sick note without examining him, and then to take it to the school principal so that his sick leave would be registered and his monthly salary secured.

This was his wish. But I do not intend to grant our hero all his desires. This is still my story. Yes, yes... I should not interfere in events, and simply narrate from a far without meddling in the details. But if you think about it, you will realize that imagination interferes ruthlessly in the creation of reality – the present, the future, and even the past. So, I will not shy away from direct interference, from time to time, in order to push things down a particular path. I will, for example, visit the principal's dreams now, before he wakes, and stimulate his mind with dreams that will cause his neurons to construct false memories about that glum-featured, slump-shouldered teacher whom he so loathed, on account of the way he sullied his respectable profession as an educator with that miserable trade he practiced in the market. The principal has hated this teacher for quite some time. All *I* am going to do is spark that dormant hatred with a false scene involving the teacher and the principal's wife, which will have him wake in a panic and ride the waves of his anger all the way to the teacher's house. I won't need any other details. The anger won't allow the principal to think of anything else, and as soon as he lays eyes on the monster that the teacher has become, he will smile triumphantly and take the administrative steps necessary to remove the teacher's name from the civil service registry, thus terminating his salary immediately.

The thought of the doctor's note and his guaranteed salary, which would remain available to the family, allowed our hero to open his archive of memories and access the record of last Thursday's events with more composure and less sadness, even if his anger had in no way diminished.

He had not expected her to fall on him with a hate-fueled slap, followed by an insult that would strip him of his honor as she stripped him of his fruit crate and threw it in her car before charging towards him, sparks of rage flying from her eyes, to kick him between the legs, sending him to the ground in a howl of pain, then following that up with a second kick to the stomach and a third to his side, before stopping, breathless, hands on hips, to look at him sprawled at her feet, moaning in pain and humiliation, then finally yelling at him again, "How dare you, you son of a bitch?"

Time stopped and all movement in the market ceased, apart from the cackles of her assistant, who laughed, and laughed, and laughed, as he pushed the fruit and vegetable cart behind the police car.

His tears caught behind his eyelids. The indignity of the slap hurt him more than the policewoman's kicks.

He lay on the ground, curled in on himself, hugging his knees to his chest and sobbing silently. He asked for nothing but the price of the fruits she took. He let his tears roll hotly down his face and into the dusty ground of the market, and the policeman's cackles echoed in his ears in an endless loop as consciousness slipped away from him little by little.

What seemed like an eon passed before he tried, sluggishly, to get up. He made it to his knees and looked around at his fellow vendors, who lowered their eyes in shame at their inability to help him. He was cocooned in despair for a sudden moment, during which he thought about getting up and going straight away to buy enough gasoline to burn himself alive in front of the Municipal palace. Then he thought of his mother and sister, who would be left without a breadwinner after him. He convinced himself that the world didn't need another Bouazizi, and dragged himself, weighed down as he was with humiliation, toward the mosque toilets to wash himself and return home to finish his lesson plans for the first days of the new school year.

The clock on the wall struck eight just as someone struck several violent knocks on the front door, and he awoke teary-eyed from his revery, wondering who this early visitor could be. He raised his eyes and pierced through the wall with his gaze to see past the door of the apartment, then trembled when he saw the principal. He yelled in a hoarse, strangled voice not to open the door.

His yell, which reached the living room like an indistinct bellow, arrived too late, after his father, who had never before done so in his life, had already gotten up and opened the door.

The principal asked to see the teacher, but the father apologized that his son was sick to the stomach, and it was in no one's best interest to see him. The principal insisted, his argument with the father becoming heated and his anger intensifying until he pushed through the door and strode into the living room and then stopped, aghast, in front of the whiteness of the teacher's wife. Only then did everyone realize, too late, that the wife was sitting in their midst in her nightgown, practically naked. With an indignant howl, the teacher overcame the pangs of numbness and stood up, grabbed the bedsheet, opened the door so forcefully he nearly ripped it from its hinges, burst into the room, and threw the sheet over his wife.

The principal turned his enraptured gaze towards the hairy, droopy-featured beast that had come storming in and, upon seeing his face, let out a shout. This was no scream of fear, but a whoop of joy. He turned on his heel and sprinted toward the door.

The father blocked the principal's way, begging and pleading with all the respect he could muster for him not to tell anyone about the curse that had befallen his son. The principal looked at the father with disgust, then turned to the son with a look of triumph, pushed past the father, and bounded out of the apartment.

Neither the mother nor the sister had grasped what had just happened, while panic appeared on the wife's face and the father stood back up and reached for the vase. Taking it in both his hands, he flung it with all his skinny, nervous might at his son's chest. It shattered, its shards burrowing into his chest and its force knocking him onto his back. The animal within him wanted to cry out in pain, but he quelled the urge, just as he had quelled his tears under the strikes of his father's belt as a child. He pulled himself together, flipped onto his side, and slunk into his room.

His wife exclaimed that she could bare it no longer and ran into the kitchen, returning with a large knife. Before anyone realized what was happening, she had entered the bedroom.

Malice beamed from her eyes as she pointed the knife at her husband, warning him not to come any closer as she stuffed clothes haphazardly into her suitcase and fastened it shut, then tucked her tall, alluring body into a tight-fitting jilbab and pulled her suitcase out behind her, still brandishing the knife.

No one dared approach her. His mother tried to calm her, but she bellowed in her face until the poor mother withdrew. His wife cast a final look of good riddance at her sick child and left the apartment.

The father didn't move a muscle, but his displeasure was evident on his face. The sister turned toward the mongoloid child and let fall the tears she'd been holding behind her eyelids. As for the husband, he fell once more to the ground, resting his back against the corner of the room and moaning faintly. The father rose and closed the door to his son's room to block out the sad, animal whine.

He could not remember when he first regretted his marriage, nor at what point he discovered that marriage was a social trap that everyone pushes you into with sadistic glee until the suffering that everyone has been concealing from the bachelors spreads to ensnare them, too. At any rate, he was obliged to marry after committing that disgraceful mistake – after that diabolic seed was sown before his marriage.

It wasn't love. But there was certainly a mutual attraction which had allowed them to pass safely through that period. He had never imagined that he would do such a thing, or that he could commit such an error. To this day, he did not know exactly what had happened. He was being treated for severe burns on his arms and chest after a teapot was spilled on him in the teachers' lounge. And she was a nurse who cared for him with utmost expertise for several days at Mohammed V Hospital. Was it loneliness, frustration, depression, anger, or a pure drive towards self-destruction? Perhaps all those raging feelings combined to lower a veil of mist over his eyes and destroy his defenses, and he surrendered himself to this woman's embrace. The only way to extinguish the fire raging within him was to let the volcano spew its lava. Yet sometimes, in moments of diabolical doubt, he thinks she pulled him into her that night to secure an alternate lifeboat for herself after the seed's true sower abandoned her.

Only a few months later, she miscarried the seed and entered a period of depression that would leave her a lifeless corpse. He astonished himself by not grieving the loss, which he considered a salvation. So, when the next pregnancy resulted in a child with Down syndrome, he immediately concluded that this was divine punishment for his repudiation and suspicion of his wife, whom he had very nearly abandoned after her miscarriage, before his sympathy got the better of him.

It was not today that she had left him, he thought, but long ago.

At some point, sleep overcame him. Or maybe he lost consciousness as he lay huddled in the corner of the room. The rest of the family remained fixed in place all morning, until the noontime prayer was called from the neighborhood mosque. The mother started, as though waking from a deep sleep. She realized she had not prepared any lunch for the family, nor had anyone even had breakfast yet. Supporting herself on the chair's armrests, she heaved herself up. But before making it all the way up, she let herself fall back into the chair and succumbed to a bout of crying, lamenting the fate of her poor son and insisting, with all the solemnity of her faith, by the honorable Grace and the immaculate Kaaba, that it was the neighbor woman who had bewitched her son after he refused to marry her daughter, whom the whole city knew was a loose woman who kept the company of all the city's men.

The father roared at her to shut up, then got up and quietly opened the door to peer in cautiously at the monster that had afflicted him since the morning. He closed the door again and turned to face his wife and daughter. "He's sleeping now. Quit your crying and fix us something to fill our stomachs." And he left to perform the noontime prayer.

The daughter tried to console her mother, reminding her that the whole mess with the neighbor's daughter was three years old. If their neighbor had really wanted to bewitch her brother, she would have already done so a long time ago. The mother paused for a moment, then resumed with fresh determination. It was his wife, then. That snake. I never trusted her. I told you before that she got pregnant before her wedding. She's a witch who tricked your kindhearted brother, and then when he no longer suited her, she turned him into a monster and ran away.

Nothing like a mother's faith, the daughter thought as she helped her mother up to prepare a bite to eat for her father before he returned from his prayers; there was no way they could bear his anger – not now, not with her brother in his room like that, with God only knows what ailment or curse.

CHAPTER 5

The Man in the High Castle

He opened his eyes and stretched his arms wide, yawning. He felt at ease. He smiled with satisfaction, knowing the pain was over and he'd finally awoken from that nightmare he'd feared might never end. A nightmare in which he'd seen himself turned into a monster, hairy and dwarfish like a demonic monkey. He inhaled, filling his mouth and nose, seeking the pleasure of air after drowning, but instead the putrid stench assailed his senses. He opened his eyes all the way and raised his palms to find two hands that were not his own. So, it wasn't a nightmare that had come to settle on his chest in the night. No, it was the reality he awoke to in the morning.

He noticed an absolute silence enveloping the house, and a phosphorescent green shading everything he looked at. He raised his eyes to the clock and saw it was close to midnight. All the lights were out. He must have slept through a whole day and half the night. He thought. He must have been unconscious – almost dead. He remembered the vase that his father had hurled at his chest, and the glass shards, and the blood dripping from his body. He tilted his head and saw bloody shards on his lap, but his chest was free of glass. He felt it with his finger, then felt it a second time, and a third. His injuries had healed completely.

He cast his vision around the apartment. He saw his sister asleep in her room, the gentle child beside her. He saw his father lying in bed, and next to him his mother, lying on her back and staring at the ceiling.

His mother's suffering made his chest tighten. He rubbed his forehead, trying to remember the details of *The Metamorphosis* and the series of events that befell Gregor Samsa. After his father had shut him in his room, Gregor had surrendered to sleep. When he awoke in the morning, he found that his injuries had healed and he was better, and his sister had made him breakfast.

Reaching that point in the story, his nose suddenly perked up. He homed in on the doorway to his room, where someone had left him food. It was no doubt his sister – he could smell her scent beside the plates.

He leapt over on all fours to sniff the plates. He pushed the boiled vegetables away in disgust and lifted the plate of meat. He drank the broth with pleasure, then put down the plate and picked up the hunk of meat with his hands, mashing it between his fingers and stuffing it into his mouth. Grease and broth dripped down his chin and from his hands to his elbows. He chewed and chewed and chewed, then swallowed and let out a great belch, then went back to lick himself from fingertips to elbows. He grabbed the water jug and drank straight from it. His face turned blue and he regurgitated, spitting over and over until he'd gotten all the water he'd drunk out of his mouth. He screamed in anger, got up and opened the bedroom window to dump out the rest of the water. Ignoring the curses that rose from the street from someone who'd been hit by the contents of the jug, he retreated inside. He made his way to the corner of the room. He loosened his pajama bottoms and held the jug below his abdomen. Several short, elated cries escaped his mouth and he let out a sigh of relief. He lifted his pajamas. He examined the yellow liquid now filling the jug to the brim, then gulped it down. He let out another tremendous belch and patted his belly with satisfaction.

He stood leaning against the window, delighting in the cool night breeze. He closed his eyes and tuned his ear to the conversations coming from the street and the neighboring apartments. The first to reached him was a girl's dirty talk whispered into a telephone as her boyfriend panted on the other end. His body trembled in ecstasy. Supporting himself on the window frame, he hoisted himself up to crouch on the ledge. He looked out at Tangier by night – a devil on his throne surveying his kingdom. He turned his head to the left and gave a satisfied smile as he directed his gaze across Avenue Belgique, then down Rue du Mexique to where it turned into Avenue M'Sallah. He saw three burly figures armed with a long knife and two clubs blocking a couple's path. They took the wife's purse, the husband's wallet, and the phones and watches of both. One still wanted a bit more, so he pulled the wife towards him, running his hands down her back. The husband tried to play the hero, which brought one of the clubs crashing down on his head over and over until it was pulp. One of them gagged the wife to silence her screams before they gathered her up and fled the scene.

The monkey in the window clapped gleefully and scratched his armpit in delight. He looked to the right, toward the tourist hotel a few meters away. Behind the curtains of one of the windows, he saw the bed rocking. He rested his chin on his fist and closed his eyes to wait a few minutes until the moaning and panting stopped.

He opened his eyes and saw the slack-bellied moaner get up and go to the bathroom. His companion stood abruptly and tucked her body into her short dress, then darted over to the other side of the bed and pulled his fat wallet out of his pants' pocket. She pulled out the bills and credit cards, tossing the passport aside after staring for a moment at the photo of him sporting a goatee and agal[1]. She balled up her underwear and stuffed it into her purse, picked up her high-heeled shoes, and left barefoot.

The monkey shook his head in amazement and blew her a kiss, then directed his gaze all the way to the right, to the end of the boulevard, where a sports car screeched to a sudden halt. The passenger door opened, and a young woman got out, wearing a mini skirt barely covering the curve of her buttocks and a belly shirt barely concealing the dark skin around her nipples. She slammed the door and cursed the driver, who got out, shouting that she was a whore. She stopped and turned back towards him to launch the insult back at his mother. He ducked into the car and came back out with a pistol. He aimed it at her chest. The woman froze. He looked terrified with the gun in his hand and seemed to be battling against some outside force for control over his own movements. He tried to loosen his grip on the gun but instead, his finger pulled the trigger. Finally, his hand relaxed and the pistol fell. He got into his car and fled as though pursued by demons.

The shot pierced the night's silence and a few lights flicked on in the windows. A few heads peered out, looking for the source of the strange noise. A few of them saw the prostitute's body crumpled on the sidewalk, but couldn't make out any details. They figured it was just a homeless person sleeping on the sidewalk – not

---

[1] A black headband worn by men in the Gulf region. It is worn over a cloth headdress, called a ghutra or shmagh, to keep it in place.

an uncommon sight in this city – or maybe some drunk who'd been kicked out of one of the neighborhood bars.

The lights shut their eyes once more and fell asleep under the wing of night, and the monkey began to slip down the windows of the building to the street, intent on a mission of which our hero will know nothing, except that when he wakes up, he will find his hands stained with blood and he won't know how it got there. A strange notion will occur to him later, when the police come to inform the family of his wife's murder, but he will immediately push the thought from his mind, for it is a diabolical notion – illogical, and utterly impossible.

Let us now leave the monkey to his mission, the teacher to his loss, the husband to his anger, and the brother to his betrayal, and come with me to see what the others are up to.

In order to make the storytelling easier for me, and easier for you to follow, I find myself obliged, at this juncture, to name the characters of our story. So, I will give our hero the name Jawad, generous as he is. The sister I'll call Hind, the mother, Fatima, and, since hope comes with daughters, his little girl I'll call Amal. There's no need to name the wife, since she will be dying soon. No, better give her the name Sara, in case I need it. As for the father, he'll be Mohammed, family name al-Idrisi.

CHAPTER 6

The Last Temptation of Christ

The mother did not sleep that night. Nor the next one, or the next, or any night following. A prolonged insomnia settled over her and did not leave until her son died. Then she let out a great sigh and fell fast asleep.

She spent the first night lying on her back next to her sleeping husband, reciting verses of supplication she had memorized, and short surahs from the Qur'an that Jawad had patiently helped her learn for her prayers. But her husband's snores kept breaking her concentration, and she would abandon her pious recitations to pray instead that a curse be brought upon her neighbor, whom she was certain had bewitched her son. Then, before getting too carried away, she would stop, ask Allah's forgiveness, and resume her supplications for his protection until her husband's snores would break her focus once again.

Her heart broke for Jawad. She tried to imagine what she would have done if he were her real son. She shook her head hysterically, trying to dislodge the thought from her mind. She clenched her teeth and muttered to herself, "It makes no difference. Jawad is my son." She remembered how the baby's wide-eyed gaze had enchanted her, how she had floated on the sea of those bright, innocent eyes.

Fatima was born in the neighborhood of Marshan, but her family's roots were in the town of Beni Boufrah, near Al Hoceima. They had come to Tangier to escape the famine[2]. They had gone first to Tetouan, where her mother worked as a maid for a Spanish family. But after a year, they packed their bags again and set off for Tangier. There, things were no better. Fatima endured a childhood of suffering, poverty, and deprivation that continued into her adolescence. So, when Mohammed al-Idrisi turned up from the same town, she agreed to the engagement without hesitation, despite the son, barely a year old, he bore in his arms. Or, to be more precise, she convinced herself that she agreed, for the truth was, her father was going to marry her off with or without her approval.

He was a widow, her fiancé had explained. His wife had passed away, leaving him with the baby Jawad. In those days, it wasn't easy to verify such claims, and Fatima would later learn that it was a lie. He wasn't a widow. He had abandoned his wife in Tetouan and taken their son, leaving the poor woman to roam the streets, sleeping on the sidewalk and asking passersby if they had seen her son Jawad. She was homeless for months, until one of the Spanish nuns found her and took her in.

Eventually, Jawad's mother would find her way to Fatima's house, and Fatima, who had suffered from years of infertility before finally conceiving her daughter Hind, would refuse to return her son to his mother. There were two reasons for this. First, she had cared for the child for three years. He was now her son, no mat-

---

[2] The Moroccan population suffered a year of famine and epidemic in 1944-1945 because of drought and measures imposed by the French protectorate on the distribution of basic foodstuffs.

ter what anyone said. And second, she was not going to hand over a Muslim child to a woman who had abandoned her faith and converted to Christianity. The first thing the father did upon his return was to grab his first wife by the hair and throw her barefoot into the street. Fatima could not accept that kind of violence from her husband towards his first wife, who was still supposed to be under his protection. Nevertheless, she remained silent, fearing he would take Jawad from her after what he'd done to his first wife. A few days later, they packed up what little furniture they had and moved to the working-class neighborhood of Bir Chairi to hide.

Tears escaped Fatima's eyes and slid down her prematurely wrinkled face. She was only forty-six, but anyone who saw her would guess she was nearly sixty. She wondered if Jawad's affliction was Allah's punishment for what she and her husband had done to that poor mother, the rightful mother of Jawad.

The dawn prayer was called, and her husband rolled over, preparing to wake up. She closed her eyes, feigning sleep, and rolled onto her side, turning her back to her husband. She stayed like that until she heard the front door close behind him as he left for the mosque. Then she got up and went to Jawad's room. She opened the door a crack and peeked in. He was asleep beneath the covers and the window was open, letting in a cool dawn breeze with hints of the sea. Even so, the stench nearly suffocated her. She plugged her nose, trying not to gag, then stepped back and closed the door.

She washed and prayed the dawn prayer, then prepared some incense and returned to her son's room to recite incantations to expel the evil from his body. Holding the incense close to her nose to overpower the room's smell, she pushed open the door. Jawad had rolled over and the sheet had slipped off him. Her heart shrank and her eyes froze on the coarse hair on his chest, his deformed legs, and drooping lips. She begged Allah for forgiveness, strength, and refuge from the accursed Satan. She approached the bed to begin her healing rituals, but dropped the incense and screamed when she saw the blood covering Jawad's hands all the way to his elbows.

Jawad's eyes snapped open, and the mother grew even more frightened when she saw the ruby red that had completely overtaken the whites of his eyes. The son opened his mouth as if to speak, gesturing something with his hands that the mother couldn't interpret. But the only sound that came out was an incomprehensible groan that could have been the snarl of an injured wild animal. The mother covered her face and buried her head in her chest. At that moment, Hind came in and saw what her mother had seen. She patted her mother's shoulder, then put her arm around her waist and guided her out.

The mother collapsed into the armchair and hugged her knees to her chest, sobbing faintly with a staccato, almost silent cry. She remained like that until the father returned from his prayers. Then she stopped crying at once. She had made up her mind what to do.

After breakfast, the father went back to sleep and the sister went to check on her brother. She stared silently at him, and he stared silently back. Then she deposited his breakfast by the door and retreated, closing the door behind her. As for the mother, she had donned her jilbab and draped her white veil over her face, then left to see a faqih[3], of whose virtues she had heard a great deal.

---

[3] The official meaning of faqīh is an Islamic jurist, an expert in fiqh (Islamic jurisprudence). In Morocco, however, it is also used to refer to people who perform healing spells with Qur'anic verses, summoning the help of jinn.

She knew she was supposed to take her bewitched son with her but, realizing this was impossible, she settled for a shirt from his dirty laundry. And so, off she went on her errand, where the faqih will assure her, with the confidence of someone who has already heard her story, that her son has been bewitched and the person behind it is a woman with ill-intentions towards her son. The charm had been placed under the doormat, he explained, where the son had stepped on it when he left the apartment and again when he returned. The ill-willed woman had then taken it and flushed it down the toilet, and by now it had reached the sea where it could never be recovered.

"So what is to be done?" The question came out hesitant and confused, spoken by a woman who wasn't used to leaving the house without her husband or son. The faqih took the bewitched young man's shirt, spat on it, then lit it on fire and let it burn on a metal plate to his left. He waited until it had burned up entirely, then got up and gathered the ashes. He mixed them with a bit of ink and spat again. Dipping a quill into the ashy mixture, he scrawled several lines on a piece of rough paper. When he had finished, he folded it carefully and placed it in an amulet, which he gave to the aggrieved mother and instructed her to place it around her son's neck or, failing that, under his pillow.

The mother got up and put a purple twenty dirham note in the faqih's hand. He shrieked and dropped the money as though it were a hot coal. He asked loudly for Allah's protection against Satan, then told her that her son's curse was a difficult one. It had required immense effort, and the Blue Jinn he served accepts only blue. The mother turned her back to fish her wallet out of her bosom and extracted a blue note, mourning the days when faqihs were content with five dirhams. And now they wanted two hundred! The faqih plucked the two-hundred-dirham note from her hand and gave her a rotten-toothed smile. "Inflation, ma'am. Even jinn suffer from inflation."

Poor Fatima would soon regret parting with all that cash after she found that the "healing" amulet in fact did just the opposite. For, when she snuck into her son's room that afternoon, thanking Allah that he was asleep again, and placed the amulet under his pillow, she saw with her own two eyes – which will one day be eaten by worms, as she would later say to a woman waiting with her to see another faqih – how his eyebrows suddenly grew in an alarming fashion. She froze for a moment in shock. Once she'd composed herself, she tried removing the amulet from under the pillow and saw, to her amazement, that his eyebrows shrunk back to their normal size. She put the amulet back, and this time saw his beard grow and grow until it was hanging off the edge of the bed. She nearly fainted but managed to remain upright and removed the amulet once more. The beard returned to normal. She decided to burn the amulet and find a new faqih. But the same sequence of events will repeat themselves with faqih after faqih, until she'll finally decide to surrender to whatever fate Allah had ordained.

CHAPTER 7

The Days (1)

Monday, August 29th: I woke up this morning to a scream piercing my eardrums and a cold steel fist clenching my heart. My first thought was that Judgment Day was upon us. But then I recognized my brother's voice buried within the growling scream. My heart practically jumped out of my chest at the next scream – a scream of animal fright, in the voice of my sister-in-law. Then the sound of something alive hitting the floor. I jumped out of bed and raced out of my room, where I found my mother also running for my brother's room. My father, meanwhile, was bent over his prayer mat, trying to kill as many skin cells as possible on his forehead in order to make his prayer bump more pronounced[4]. We pounded on the door, but no one answered. Mama's face was covered with tears and I swear I could practically hear her heart racing in her chest. I had such an adrenaline rush, I felt like I'd gained super powers. I grabbed the door handle and I'm sure I could have forced it open

---

[4] The prayer bump, called zabibat al-salah, or "prayer raisin" in Arabic, is a callous that sometimes develops on the forehead from repeatedly touching one's forehead to the ground in prayer. Some regard it as a mark of devotion, while others consider it a form of performative piety.

with my bare sweaty hand if my father hadn't come along right then with the spare key. Luckily, it's the kind of lock you can unlock from the outside even if the other key's inside. When the door swung open, a burst of hot, stinky air hit me in the face like a ghoul's breath. Or a hyena's burp. Or maybe the stale air of a Pharoah's tomb… I took a step back and my father went in first. My sister-in-law was sprawled on the floor. I couldn't tell if she was dead or just unconscious. I noticed how my father's eyes lingered on her tits, which were popping out of her nightgown. Once I went further into the room a dark figure in the corner of the room caught my eye. At first it looked like a monkey in pants. Then I blinked and it looked like a goat sitting on its haunches. I blinked again and it looked like a human dwarf completely covered in hair, with the face of my dear brother. Then my vision clouded and the ground started spinning and then slammed against me. Mama screamed. I felt her fingertips grappling around my neck. The black cloud cleared from my vision, and I opened my eyes. I could hear my mother crying in the living room. My sister-in-law was gone. I struggled to get up. I felt exhausted. Like one of Azkaban's Dementors was crouching on top of me. My eyes landed on my brother's face in the corner of the room where he was huddled. A chill ran down my spine and I felt sparks of electricity jumping from the floor to my toes. The smell made me feel dizzy and faint. I don't know how to describe it other than as a satanic smell. No. It's literally the smell of Satan himself. My dear father finally remembered me and came back to help me up and out of my brother's room. He closed the door behind me. I lay down on the sofa next to Mama, who was rocking my poor little niece. The baby was born with what people call "Mongolian idiocy." The baby's mother was hugging her legs and staring off into another world. I'm positive she was trying to come up with the best way to finally escape from her marriage, and from that daughter she could never stand. I have no clue what attracted my brother to that woman. She's arrogant and materialistic through and through. Mama says that she got pregnant before the marriage and that's the only reason my brother rushed into marrying that spotted snake. I've tried to get the idea out of my mother's head, so her tongue doesn't one day slip in front of the wrong person, but I'm also convinced that it was her dirty pregnancy that entrapped my brother, and it was the only thing that made him stay with that vacuous woman who treats this house like a hotel and our family like servants. Sadly, she did not prove me wrong today. After an hour and a half, just as the clock struck eight, we heard someone at the front door. It was the principal from my brother's school. When he pushed his way in passed my protesting father and saw what had befallen my brother, his face lit up and he left, practically jumping with joy. When I saw my serpent-in-law's reaction, I understood why the principal was pleased by my brother's misfortune. This was his golden opportunity to fire him from the school. She had caught on immediately and started fake-screaming as she got up, gathered her things, and left, running away from her husband when he needed her most, just like she'd been running away from taking care of her miserable daughter since the day she was born. The rest of the day went by, somehow, and a silence fell over us like a graveyard in the afternoon. The three of us sat in the living room together, all lost in our own private thoughts. Little Amal finally calmed down and fell asleep. My brother, too, stopped his heartbreaking, howling moans and slept. No one's said a single word the whole day about what's happened to my brother. We somehow reached an unspoken agreement to swallow our shock and digest it slowly, silently, without sharing our thoughts with each other.

Tuesday, August 30th: It's the second day in a row I'm woken up by a scream. Last night, before I fell asleep, I hoped I'd wake up in the morning to find it had all been a bad dream. But the scream in Mama's voice killed that hope in my heart. I jumped out of bed to see what had happened this time. Ya Allah! What a smell. It smells like death. How can my poor brother stand it? On my way in, I noticed that the plate of meat I left him last night was empty. That made me happy. Then I saw why my mother had screamed. I can't imagine why my brother's arms were covered in blood. I guided my mother out, but on my way, I picked up the book lying on the floor by the bed. Something about its strange title grabbed me: *The Metamorphosis*. I'll go back soon to bring my brother his breakfast. I left the door open and pulled up the window shades and sprayed some perfume in the air, but the smell has seeped into the room and won't leave. I couldn't stay in there long. I was afraid my heart would jump out of my throat along with everything in my stomach. My father's gone back to sleep and Mama's gone out, which isn't like her. I fed Amal and played with her a bit, then did some housework. Then I started getting my school supplies together, since we're starting up again next week. Jawad hasn't left his room since yesterday, not even to use the bathroom. Where is he answering "nature's call?" Yuck. It's making my stomach turn – is he doing it in his bedroom? In his bed?! I'm the one who's going to have to clean it up, wherever it is. I know mama won't be able to handle it, what with all her diseases. I'll deal with it. Really, it's nothing compared to all my brother's done for me. If he didn't give up his own dreams to take care of our family after our father stopped doing anything for us, I wouldn't be able to keep studying.

My father has implied more than once that there's no need for a woman to study. Sooner or later a man will come for her. Until then, better for her to go find a job, any job, and bring her salary every month and place it in her father's lap and ask for his blessing. Whatever I do, I'll never be able to pay back Jawad the Generous. The generous never get what they deserve.

Wednesday, August 31st: I didn't sleep at all last night. I couldn't stop crying. What I'd been afraid of actually happened. We'd just sat down to dinner and hardly taken a few bites, when my father suddenly turned to me. He said I'd studied long enough and learned everything I need. He thinks a high school degree and a year at university is plenty – no need for a bachelor's degree. He says he's fulfilled his duties to the family long ago and now it's my turn to take care of the family, seeing as my brother's stopped doing it. Then he threw an envelope down on the table and said that my brother's name has been permanently struck from the list of government employees. No more salary, no retirement fund – and no compensation to speak of. No way. That fast? Ya Allah, look how efficient Moroccan bureaucracy can be when it wants to be! So my father says I should start working. Apparently, he ran into an old friend recently who used to work with him when he was bartending, who's now opened a fancy café overlooking Mallabata Beach. He muttered something about how this guy only has the money for his project because he got into the drug trade. He was obviously jealous, and not even trying to hide it. Then he looked at me again and told me his friend agreed to give me a job as a waitress in his café, and I could start tomorrow. Mama started slapping her face and beating her chest in dismay. I swallowed hard and got up. I felt like I'd been drugged. I tried to make it to my room even though I could barely see through my tears. But my father grabbed me by the hair and pulled me back to the table and shouted at me that I was to sit and keep eating until he gave me permission to leave. When I woke up this morning, my eyes were red from crying and lack of sleep. I'd better shower quickly and get to the café to start my new job.

Wednesday, August 31st (evening): I'm back home now. My shift ended mid-afternoon. My feet were killing me by the end and my manager told me I'll have to get sneakers for this kind of work, since I have to be on my feet for hours at a time. My manager is nice, but my first day was exhausting. And I'm not even really working yet, just training. I peaked in on my brother as soon as I got home. He was crouched in the corner of the room with his eyes closed like he was meditating or something. He opened his eyes when I went in and a smile spread across his face, even though I could barely see it, what with his thick mustache and beard and drooping lips. But I returned his smile and put the minced meat sandwich I'd brought back from the café for him on the bed. I went to shower then came out to bury myself in my mother's arms. We cried together silently until we heard Amal crying. I changed her and warmed her up some milk.

Thursday, September 1st: Before going to sleep last night, I read the story of *The Metamorphis* that I took from my brother's room. My goodness – it's so much like everything that's happening to us right now! Sometimes almost word for word. And now I'm afraid the ending will be the same too. It's a story about Gregor Samsa – traveling salesman, self-sacrificing young bachelor who gave up on his dreams to support his family – a father, a mother, and a little sister – after his father lost his business and started drowning in debt. The young man was forced into working a job he didn't like to save his family from poverty. But one morning, he woke up to find himself turned into a monster. A giant insect. That day, everything changed for the family. First, because Gregor was late for work, his boss sent someone to enquire after him. And so his metamorphosis was discovered, which led to him losing his job and his family's only source of income. His parents had a hard time processing the metamorphosis. His father was rough with him, and when he pushed him into his room on the first morning, he broke one of his son's many legs. Only the sister took care of her brother, bringing him leftovers of different dishes so he could choose what he liked, and cleaning his room for him. Because the maid and the cook had fled, it also fell to the sister to take on the housework alongside her mother. Then the mother had to start working as a seamstress from home, and the father had to find a job. After a few days, the sister noticed that her brother the insect liked to crawl around the room and on the walls. She thought it would make sense to clear out some of the furniture he no longer needed, to give him more space to roam about. At first the brother was happy, but the little bit of humanity that still coursed through his veins led him to climb the wall and cling to his favorite painting, to keep her from taking it from him. When the mother and sister returned to his room after carrying out a box of his clothes, his mother saw him clinging to the wall and was so frightened, she fainted. His sister went to find something to revive her mother with, and her insect brother followed her out. Just then, the father returned from work and saw that his wife had passed out and the insect had upset a water jug. He started hurling apples at the insect to get him back to his room. The insect was so large that it was difficult for him to turn around, so he suffered several more blows from the flying apples as he made his way back to his room. One of the apples pierced his back, which really hurt. Finally, Gregor was able to retreat to his room, where he passed out from the pain. The apple stayed in his back and started rotting and making him sicker and sicker, especially because he stopped eating and began growing weak. The sister started working too, and stopped taking care of her brother, who by now could hardly move. Later on, three men would come to rent a room in the apartment and the family would become their servants. One day, after dinner, the sister picked up her violin and began playing for the tenants. Gregor had always adored his sister's playing and had set aside money for her to attend lessons at the music institute. Enchanted by her playing, which he'd really missed, he came out of his bedroom, forgetting all about the three strange men who, as soon as they saw him, started fuming, threatening to prosecute the head of the family and saying they wouldn't pay their rent, because he was harboring an insect in the house. The tenants left, and in a moment of anger, the sister said the time had come to get rid of the insect. This insect wasn't her dear brother at all, she said. If her brother had still been somewhere inside the insect, he would have been ashamed of himself and left a long time ago, to spare the family all this suffering. That night, Gregor decided that the only solution was indeed for him to disappear. Early the next morning, he died. The family awoke to the joyful news. The three of them decided to take the day off work and go to the countryside to enjoy some fresh air. On their outing, the parents noticed how grown up their daughter had become, and that she would make a beautiful bride.

I just got interrupted from my story by a text from Aymen. He was wondering why I haven't been in class and if we can meet. I couldn't stop thinking about Kafka's strange story and how much like my family's story it is. I wrote back to him and told him that I can't go out today because we're having guests. He asked me who they were, so I told him they were distant relatives coming to arrange my engagement. He replied with the emoji of a face slapping its cheeks and then a crying emoji. I asked him what was wrong. He reminded me that we were in love. I told him the matter's out of my hands, but that my dad would definitely approve of his family, and I could stall for a few days if he came to ask for my hand before the weekend. But he stopped responding. My trick didn't work on him.

Friday, September 2nd: At breakfast today, I told my father about my idea for earning some extra income for the family that would allow me to go back to school. There's this website where you can rent out rooms, and we have an extra guest bedroom. I showed him how the site works and how easy it is to use. He was excited about the idea, but gave the condition that we would only rent to foreign tourists. No Moroccans. And also that we would register the account with his phone number so that he could communicate directly with renters on his cell phone and not have to use email. Step one: complete.

CHAPTER 8

A Thousand and One Nights

Once upon a time there was, or there wasn't,[5] a kindhearted individual named Jawad. One morning, he awoke to find himself transformed, as though possessed by demons, into a monster – a filthy, unwelcome monster. Once upon a time, there was a kindhearted individual named Jawad who gave up his dreams and ambitions in order to provide for his family, who knew precisely when he would die, and knew he would die for his family's sake.

The day following his metamorphosis, Jawad awoke to his mother's scream and the clatter of her incense holder hitting the ground. He opened his eyes and saw fear etched into her wrinkly face and a sea of pain in her eyes. Frightened, he sat up. He wiped his hands furiously on his pajamas. He was relieved when the blood came off and he realized it was not his own, but then was all the more frightened by the thought of where the blood might have come from.

---

[5] This chapter begins, in the Arabic, with kan ya ma kan, a phrase which, like "once upon a time," is used by Scheherazade and other storytellers at the beginning of their tales. Its literal meaning, "there was, or there wasn't," signal to listeners that what they are about to hear may be truth, or fancy, or some of both.

His head ached terribly. He pressed his fists into his temples and closed his eyes. Then he wrapped his arms around his head, curled his knees up to his face, and let himself fall sideways onto the bed. It took all his might not to cry out in pain. He bit his lip to silence himself and began shaking and trembling. Several minutes went by before the seizure stopped as suddenly as it had started. He lay on his back, face covered in sweat, spittle dripping down his cheeks. He noticed broth stains on his pants but had no memory of the meal they'd come from. In fact, he realized he could remember nothing at all that had happened after yesterday morning's events.

He saw Hind coming, so he sat upright again and pulled the covers over himself. She entered and deposited his breakfast by the door. Then she drew the curtains to let in the fresh breeze and sprayed the air with perfume. He could sense her racing heart and bated breath, and how she gulped in air as soon as she left. He didn't try to speak to her or interfere. He did try to produce a word of thanks when she reached the door, but it came out too late, after she'd already left and closed the door.

The rest of Jawad's days will pass in much the same way. He will awake to find he can remember nothing beyond the morning hours of the previous day. Everything he did after that will have vanished from his memory completely. Yet he wakes up in the morning exhausted, as though he's spent the night performing manual labor. Sometimes he wakes up wearing clothes he has no memory of putting on, or finds strange marks and scratches on his hands that he couldn't possibly have gotten without leaving the house. And yet, he's sure he hasn't even left his bedroom.

Despite the cloud of mystery hanging about him, he is sometimes filled with a feeling of blissful calm. He begins to feel a new kind of freedom. This newfound freedom from any responsibility to his family leaves him as light as a butterfly in springtime, flitting from flower to perfumed flower. But such thoughts are always followed by guilt, and he casts them aside whenever he sees his mother's grief and exhaustion, plodding from faqih to quack faqih. Or whenever his sister returns from work after their father forbade her from attending university. From his room, he sees the harassment she endures at the café – how one day a customer ogled the youthful breasts peeking out of her work uniform, and how that same customer, just before leaving, wrote his number on a blue bank note and tucked it into her cleavage. He swore he would cut off those fingers that had felt up his sister's chest. That night, he dreamed he did just that. Another day, he saw a customer grab the waitress's ass and then laugh, as though he were just having fun with her. So, he promised to cut off that hand, and he had no doubt he really would.

It pained him to see what his sister endured, though he was sometimes plagued by the nagging thought that she was somehow bringing these situations upon herself. But then he would push that thought away and recall his graceful, kind sister – the nimble butterfly, the diligent student, the promising writer. Suddenly he remembered her latest short story, which she'd given to him to read and give his opinion on. That had been before his curse made him forget all about it. He got up excitedly and retrieved the story from his desk drawer. He contemplated the title for a moment – "the Sands War"[6] – and then started reading:

---

[6] The Sands War was a conflict between Morocco and Algeria that took place in October, 1963, over dispute of border territories. It led to lasting tensions between the two countries.

We heard the gunshot and watched us fall.

We had spent the night out in the open, wrapped in a blanket of stars, under the icy desert sky. We were in a race against time, building the wall of sand day and night and we watched ourselves from the other side day and night building the wall of sand.

We came from the University of Oran and we came from Mohammed V University. We came sporting our lieutenant's badges from the Royal Military Academy we came sporting our lieutenant's badges from the Combined Arms Military School we volunteered from the streets of Annaba and Rabat and Setif and Tlemcen and Fes and Marrakesh we were taken by force from our houses in Tangier and Tetouan and Kasantina and Batna and Agadir.

We heard the gunshot and watched us fall. Fall all at once. Fall as one of the Arab poets once said "like a mighty boulder the torrent has washed down from the heights."[7]

It was our first day here and the sun's thorns scratched our still-tender skin. It was our fifth year here and the sun tanned our faces and the desert cracked our palms and the sand tilled furrows in the soles of our feet.

We grew feverish and vomited through the night. We vomited when the mines exploded and sent our feet flying we vomited when our bullets hit our hearts we vomited when we buried our bodies left behind by their souls we vomited when we ate our ex-

---

[7] The "Arab poet" here is 6th-century poet Imru' al-Qais, and the line is from his muallaqah, one of the seven "hanging odes" of pre-Islamic poetry, which are among the best-known and -loved verses of Arabic literature. The English translation is by Suzanne Pinckney Stetkevych.

pired foods we vomited when the scorpions stung us and snakes bit us.

We grew feverish and stayed up all night shivering. We shivered when our fingers touched the cold of our guns for the first time we shivered when we touched them for the tenth time and did not feel their cold.

We talked about our sweethearts waiting in the college auditoriums our pregnant wives waiting in our parents' houses our sleepless mothers whispering prayers in the night to the creator of night and day to return us to them in one piece. We talked about Camus and al-Bayati and al-Sayyab and Nazik al-Malaika and Bint al-Shati' and al-Aqqad and Taha Hussein. We talked about makes and models and horsepower. We talked about football and hashish and dominoes and card games in the sleepless cafes by night.

We stood there laughing stood there crying stood there bruised stood there hoping stood there praying. We stood there as we fired our bullets and fell. One moment we were standing there the next fell to the ground. We pulled a single lever and the body fell all at once. It was and then it wasn't.

We grabbed a fistful of sand and let it run through our fingers like a mirage we fixed our eyes on the red twilight into the sun drowning in her own blood.

We said we would finish our studies when the war was over said we would return to our fields and to our mothers' breast and the alleyway gossip we said we would get our degrees at the finest military colleges in England and America said we would go back to start our own businesses we would go back and write a book about the ugliness of war and poems about the savagery of war and stories about the absurdity of war that would begin at the moment we heard the shot and watched us fall and would end with us scattering before the sinking sun a fistful of sand slipping from our fingers.

He read her story quickly, then went back to the beginning and read it again. He wasn't usually so inclined towards stories that waded into experimentalism and drowned themselves in symbolism. But here, he thought the topic called for this kind of expression. The chaos of war. Wars without winners or losers. Wars without angels or devils. Everyone loses, aside from those few who trade in the misery of others, amassing wealth and climbing the rungs of power.

He set down the story and closed his eyes with a sigh. He'd brought his sister whatever books she wanted, and several months ago he'd begun setting aside part of his own savings to be able to register her in a novel-writing workshop. He'd been planning it as a gift for her next birthday. But the winds don't blow where the ship desires.

Once upon a time there was, or there wasn't, a kindhearted young man named Jawad who turned into a hairy, monkey-like dwarf and was locked in his room, which he believed he had not left since the curse had struck him.

Most of the mornings he could recall were the same: he opens his eyes and checks his extremities to see if anything has changed. Three months go by, and nothing does. Not even a single hair grows longer on his hirsute form. He retrieves the empty glass jug from under the bed and fills it to the brim, then gulps down the yellow liquid as usual. He does this once a day for three months. He drinks no other liquid, but each morning he fills the jug to the brim. After that, he gets up and goes to the door to eat the breakfast his sister has left for him. In the beginning, she would bring him a glass of milk like he always used to like, but he can no longer stomach it. He eats the egg and cheese and slices of smoked meat. For a while, his sister would leave him the leftover bones and fatty bits of meat from their dinner as well. But as the days pass and she grows tired from the responsibilities that have fallen on her shoulders, she begins to lag in her service to her brother. Sometimes she wakes up late and runs straight to work without preparing breakfast for him or herself. She'd begun to prefer the free breakfast she can get at the café. Sometimes she returns home in the afternoon exhausted and goes straight to bed, not getting up until the next morning. He doesn't complain. He sometimes hears his belly grumbling in complaint, but his hunger is always gone by the next morning, and he wakes up feeling satiated. After breakfast, he opens his closet and squats there for a few minutes. One of the things that his sister puzzles over, without every finding an explanation, is that the terrible smell that fills the room with such insistence never escapes through the bedroom door or window, and you can't smell it at all outside the room even when the door is open.

He wakes up feeling not just drained, but empty. It feels as though some fundamental part of himself has gone missing – melted away and evaporated. After feeding himself and relieving himself, Jawad goes back to bed and lies on his back. Sometimes he mutters to himself in vague words which reach the living room in a low buzz without anyone being able to make out a single word, and sometimes he occupies himself by painting the ceiling with streams of multi-colored spit, which he loudly launches until his father gets annoyed by the sound and comes to knock on the door and yell at the devil within to be quiet. Usually, Jawad will stop immediately, but every so often he puts on a mocking smile and continues his game. Sometimes, he'll remember his favorite hobby. He'll go to his desk to pull out the panels he decorated with calligraphy and, filled with nostalgia, read the verses of poetry he'd drawn there every time he found one he loved, and the sayings and aphorisms he'd memorized as a child. Sometimes he takes out a fresh piece of white paper and grabs a pen. Then he freezes in front of the page, not daring to let his hand budge. A tear falls onto the page so he grabs it, balling the paper in his fist, tearing it up and throwing the pieces over his should, then goes back to bed to practice one of his new favorite hobbies – spitting, or mumbling in his strange language, or singing songs from his childhood, rewriting their lyrics to rid them of all their moralizing content.

Later, after his father starts renting out the spare room next to Jawad's to foreigners, he discovers a new hobby: focusing his gaze on the wall between them to see what their guest was up to. He enjoys this the most when it is a husband and wife (at least supposedly – his father never bothers to ask for marriage papers). They're Christians, his father says, as he says of all foreigners, before adding that they're animals, so the men can sleep with their wives or their lovers or their whores or even their sisters for all he cares.

On the weeks when Hind works the evening shift, she wakes up in the morning radiant and energetic, belting out her favorite songs as she helps her mother around the house. This grows increasingly rare as a permanent frown begins to overtake her countenance, never to leave. But on the days she does sing, Jawad sits in bed, snapping his fingers to close the window against the bustle of the street, and closes his eyes to enjoy his sister's magical voice. He feels then, as he floats in the clouds, that he has regained that part of himself he'd lost, and that the void inside himself shrinks. He also feels this when his mother sits after breakfast in her favorite armchair, folding her legs under her and lacing her fingers as she recites the short surahs he helped her memorize, in a faltering voice that robs him of his smile and stirs his memories and fills him with longing. And that longing fills the emptiness that has taken over his insides, and two tears fall from his eyes, which he quickly brushes away and lies down to resume his game of spitting at the ceiling, now with his hands over his ears to block out the sound of his mother's recitations.

CHAPTER 9

Memory in the Flesh

Mohammed al-Idrisi was ten years old when he ran away from home – and from his whole village. He'd been fatherless since he was four. He had hardly any memory of the man who'd been killed in one of those army skirmishes that broke out outside of Al Hoceima following the Rif Revolt, which the army had squashed nine years earlier. The father died without getting to see his son through childhood, and it was only a matter of months before the mother had remarried to a widower with two sons of his own, whom she raised alongside Mohammed. Later, little Mohammed started hearing the rumors about his mother's new husband – that in a fit of rage, he had beaten his first wife until she died in his arms. The adults said it was nothing but talk, but Mohammed knew all too well that it was the truth and nothing but the truth. For six long years he endured his stepfather's violence, until he could take it no longer.

Mohammed al-Idrisi was ten years old when he was awoken by his mother's sobs. He knew that once again, her husband was to blame. He waited until close to dawn, when he saw his mother get up and, with a slight limp, go to milk their only cow and prepare breakfast. Then, without hesitation, he got up and went to the kitchen. He got out the biggest knife they had, the one they used for slaughtering sheep, and headed towards his mother and stepfather's bedroom. The potbellied husband lay on his back, snoring. The boy paused at the door. He faltered for a moment and almost retreated. But he stuck to his plan and crept forward until he reached his stepfather's head. Clasping the knife between his two small hands, he plunged it into the man's neck, throwing all his weight behind it. The man spluttered and blood splattered onto the boy's face. The husband reached to pull the knife out with his left hand, while reaching for Mohammed's throat with his right. His death throes did not prevent him from wringing the boy's neck. Mohammed felt himself suffocating as he clawed uselessly with his small fingers at the man's formidable arm. Just then his mother appeared and saw her eldest son suffocating under the grip of her husband's brutish fingers. She didn't stop to think. She raised her right foot and brought it down, with all the anguish she'd accumulated over the past six years, onto his stomach. He gasped silently, another fountain of blood spurted from the wound in his neck, and his grip on Mohammed's throat relaxed.

Mohammed al-Idrisi was ten years old when he ran away from home and from his whole village. Little Mohammed, stumbling over the gruesome nightmares that haunted him, reached Tetouan without any trouble. No one blocked his path as he made the brutal, two-week trek barefoot. He did not suffer from lack of food, which he easily acquired from people in the villages scattered along the way, nor from lack of sleep. Nonetheless, he reached Tetouan with depleted strength, torn clothes, cracked feet, bloodied hands, and a blackened, frowning face. He was so tired, he collapsed at the city gates and awoke inside a house, to the sound of Spanish voices. He soon learned that he'd been taken to a home for abandoned children, run by the Church of Our Lady of Victory. The Church had officially started its activities in the country just days after al-Khattabi's army was defeated by Spain and its allies: France's strongest foreign legions fought alongside the local tribes vying with al-Khattabi for power, while Spain dropped mustard gas bombs on the people of Al Hoceima, leaving them with the cancerous legacy of Spain's illegal chemical weapons. Though of course, Spain would never acknowledge this.

Mohammed al-Idrisi would stay at the church for two years, where he would learn to read and write in Spanish and tell stories from the Bible by heart. After only a few days, everyone had dropped his first name and made do with calling him al-Idrisi. Apparently, no one knew the name's connection to the Prophet's family tree, otherwise they would have dropped the last name too and found him a new one. At first, they did try to rename him, but he would not respond to anything other than al-Idrisi. He remained feisty and rebellious throughout his two-year stay. He did not perform Muslim prayers, of course, but he also never set foot near the church pews. He was content to stay in the classroom with his Bible stories and, come Sunday morning, he was nowhere to be seen. How often they thought about getting rid of him, and oh how often they shook their heads at this lost cause.

On one of those Sunday mornings when he'd fled the church, the priest intercepted him at the doorway as he was coming back. He grabbed Mohammed by the ear and pulled so hard, the boy had to stand on his tiptoes. He shouted at him, calling him a filthy infidel and a dirty Muslim. At that moment, the faqih from the local mosque was passing through the alley and heard everything. He rushed over and pulled Mohammed towards him, pointing his finger at the priest in warning. He was taking the boy with him, he said. The priest shrugged indifferently, then muttered that filth deserved to live with filth, and they had no need for him here anyway.

So off Mohammed went with the faqih, in whose care he would remain for the next several years, until the faqih married. The boy went on to memorize portions of the Qur'an — indeed, to memorize it almost in its entirety, though he would forget most of it as the years went by. He learned to read and write in Arabic, though he held onto his Spanish as well, which he would later employ as he wandered the side streets and alleys of Tetouan and Tangier.

The faqih came from one of the Jbala tribes of Tangier and had settled in Tetouan as a boy. There was a history of animosity between the northwestern Jbala tribes and the northeastern Riffian tribes to which the young Mohammed belonged. But Mohammed didn't know and the faqih didn't care.

Three years went by, during which time the faqih treated the little one, who remained little even as the fuzz on his upper lip began to darken, as the brother he'd never had. The poor thing had no idea what a nightmare fate had in store for him.

In Tetouan, the young faqih established himself as an imam in the local mosque and a teacher to the neighborhood boys and girls, teaching them to recite the Qur'an and a bit of grammar and poetry. He was a model of righteousness in the neighborhood and loved by all. And so it was that Hajj Masoud, one of the city's notables and owner of the largest spice shop in town, stayed after the evening prayer one day, waiting for the others to leave, then approached the faqih, shook his hand and, with a bowed head and a stutter, asked if he would consider marrying his daughter. The faqih was tongue-tied with surprise and didn't know what to say. He knew Hajj Masoud and his righteousness well and had heard tell of his daughters' beauty and their righteousness, too. What he did not know was that many suitors had come for the two younger daughters, but the father refused to let them marry before their elder sister. The faqih stuttered a reply, saying he hadn't yet thought of marriage because he wasn't in a financial position to do so. The Hajj offered to cover all expenses. After some hesitation, the faqih agreed, saying it would be an honor to become a member of Hajj Masoud's family, but he insisted on marrying by his own means. He would accept no help from his father-in-law and no extravagance in the wedding. The Hajj let out a sigh and readily agreed.

CHAPTER 10

Chaos of the Senses

You know what will happen, of course. The couple will spend a few happy days together. But if the story were only a matter of happy days, there'd be no reason in telling it and I wouldn't have bothered with the story of the faqih. So you've no doubt surmised that catastrophe is around the corner.

Now, perhaps you recall the story of Aziz's wife, who tried to seduce the young Prophet Yusuf?[8] Well, that is what happened here, just so. Okay, perhaps not *just so*. When the faqih arrived, the door was not bolted and he did not find a young man with a shirt torn from behind. Instead, he walked in to see his wife's behind as she straddled the soft-bodied teenager who lay on their bed crying with pleasure.

---

[8] The story of Yusuf (or Joseph) appears in the Qur'an and the Bible. The wife of Yusuf's master Aziz (the biblical Potiphar) one day bolts the door behind Yusuf and tries to seduce him. When Yusuf runs for the door, she grabs his shirt from behind, tearing it. At the door, they meet her husband. Aziz threatens Yusuf, who says that it was she who tried to seduce him. To determine who is at fault, one of her family members suggests, "If his shirt is torn from the front, then she is telling the truth and he is lying. But if his shirt is torn from behind, then she is lying and he is telling the truth" (Qur'an 12:29, tr. Tarif Khalidi).

The poor faqih did not kill the young Mohammed. Otherwise, how could he have grown up, married, and fathered the hero of our story, Jawad, who is the reason you now sit before me listening to my tale? He did not scream or protest. He did not say anything at all. He froze, yes he did. His jaw went slack, yes it did. Drool dribbled down his chin, yes it did. His eyes rolled back in their sockets, yes they did. And, what next? The faqih turned around, in all his rural naivete, and left. He was never to return to that house, and his wits were never to return to him. Weeks later, he would be seen wandering the city's side streets, silent and wide-eyed, as though in a daze. Someone recognized him and took him by the hand to lead him home. He followed along without putting up a fight until they neared his front door. Then he began kicking and screaming and ran off again. This happened several times before his neighbors gave up and doubt began to tickle the backs of their minds.

Meanwhile, the faqih's wife continued inviting the teenage boy over, sometimes several times a day, until one day she moaned too loudly and the neighbors caught on. In the face of this scandal, the only solution Hajj Masoud could see was in a bullet from his rabbit-hunting rifle. And so his daughter became the last rabbit he would hunt. After that, he never left his house again.

As for the teenager, Mohammed al-Idrisi, he'd been taken in by the faqih's wife, who had flung open the door to his whims and fancies and not closed it behind her. So, the windows of his body remained open and his nose soon caught the scent of Spanish women. When they could no longer fulfill his growing needs, he found his way to the brothels of Ceuta, then to its bars, where he began to work, hopping from bar to café and café to bar, from Ceuta to Tetouan and Tangier, going and coming during seven years of total freedom, until he was struck all of a sudden by Cupid's arrow. His captor was a young woman whose face bore the marks of Moroccan beauty, haunted by memories of al-Andalus. He was working at the time as a waiter at a hotel café in downtown Tetouan. The fatherless girl's mother agreed immediately to al-Idrisi's proposal, let out a sigh of relief, and went to sleep for the first time in years without worrying about who would take care of her daughter.

Only months after his wife had given birth to their first-born, Jawad, their love faded and he returned to his old ways, letting his nose lead him one day to an older woman, the next to a young one, and so on until word reached his wife. The ensuing argument ended with a blow so violent it knocked her unconscious. When she came to, she found her son gone, and her husband, too.

For several months, he and his baby boy were guests of a Spanish diplomat's wife in Tangier. Her husband had left as soon as his term in Morocco was up, but his wife had fallen under Tangier's spell and refused to go with him. Mohammed's new mistress gave him everything he desired and looked after his child, but one day her patience ran out and she told him that if he didn't find a solution to his son's nightly crying, one of these days she was going to throw him out of the window.

A few days later, Fatima caught his eye and he decided he wanted her as the mother of his child. It wasn't that he simply wanted to take advantage of her innocence. He really did like her. The sight of her made his heart flutter. Moreover, and this was more than he had ever expected, she made him forget his Spanish mistress and all the other girls hidden away in low houses down narrow alleys. They settled in Tangier. He got a good job and they were able to lead a comfortable life. Within a few years, he'd saved up enough money to buy a big apartment downtown. He felt that, for the first time, life was smiling upon him. And for a long time, that was enough for him. For nearly twenty years, he led an honest life and was faithful to his wife. But then, someone came along who seduced him once again.

CHAPTER 11

Bed Hopper, or the Dust of Promises

He was by no means handsome. He was, as I've said, skinny and irritable. But his eyes had a certain charm that drew women to him.

If the 20th of February, 2011, represented, for many Moroccans, the squandered opportunity when the buds of the Moroccan Spring might have bloomed and the train of comprehensive reform could have finally left the station, full steam ahead, it was, for Mohammed, the day he said goodbye to his work at the bar and shut himself up in his house for good.

That evening, the French proprietor had come in accompanied, for the first time, by her daughter – that blossoming rose of seventeen Springs. Mohammed was working the bar when they walked in, so he brought the boss her glass of cognac, which she always opened her evenings with whenever she came in, and the glass of orange juice she'd ordered for her daughter, despite her protests. That evening, his colleagues kept winking at him and nodding towards the young woman, who'd fixed her gaze on him as he made his way back and forth. And, that evening, the young woman followed him with her gaze until he went to the bathroom, then got up and followed him in, bolted the door behind them, and let her dress slip to the floor.

He did nothing.

His heart raced, but he did nothing.

Yes, he desired her, but he did nothing.

A green bird alighted on the bathroom windowsill, and he noticed how its eyes shone like Fatima's. He felt his water flow and the earth tremble beneath him. Then he fainted.

That evening was his last shift at the bar or at any other job. He sat in the house, immersing himself in worship. If you were to ask him about it, you wouldn't get an answer – not about the bird or the fainting or how either of them led to his flight to the prayer mat.

Two whole years went by, and he forgot about his old life entirely. He was to remain a captive of his prayer mat until another evening came along when he would find himself before a woman's naked body, this time dripping with water. And this time there would be no green bird with eyes shining like Fatima's.

CHAPTER 12

The Days (2)

Sunday, September 11th: I can't take it anymore. Allah, why are you punishing me like this? Isn't it enough that I wear myself out at the café and then come home to find a load of housework waiting for me? Not to mention playing maid to our tenants. And all this on top of taking care of that monster with his evil smell, which just about kills me every time I open the door. And now you send Aymen and his friends to mock me? Aymen, the boy who'd promised to marry me as soon as we finished school, now brings his friends to ridicule the valedictorian who used to be better than all of them, and who's now stuck waiting tables in a cafe. Fine. I can take that. But then to come back with a new girlfriend just to taunt me? That whore. Her tight leather pants were practically begging for mercy as they struggled to contain her ass. And her buttons were threatening to pop off her blouse like bullets. As if *that* wasn't enough. But no. As soon as Aymen left, my sister-in-law showed up. I've had it. Ya Allah, I can't stand it anymore. If only you would send me a husband to get me out of this misery.

Monday, September 12th: A detective and his team from the police department showed up today, asking after Jawad. My father let them in and asked what they were looking for. They insisted on seeing Jawad, so he showed them to my brother's room. They looked all over the room and stared at Jawad in disgust. Then they left, grimacing. Before leaving, the detective informed us that they had found Jawad's wife murdered, along with the owner of the apartment where she'd been found. I received the news coldly, as though it didn't concern me at all. I wasn't surprised. I felt like I'd been expecting it all along.

CHAPTER 13

Eleven Minutes

Hind couldn't believe her eyes. She had been leaning on the café counter sipping tea, watching the door, when her brother's wife Sara walked in, arm-in-arm with another man. She looked different, with her hair tied back and lips painted a deep red, wearing a low-cut blouse and tight jeans that showed off her curves. Hind froze. Probably the entire café could hear her heart pounding.

Hind didn't snap out of it until one of the waiters nudged her to tell her that her table's order was ready. She picked up the tray and took the long way around to her customer. She wanted to pass by Sara's table, "accidentally" trip, and spill a glass of juice on her. But in her flustered state, she tripped too soon. The glass spilled on the tray and only a few drops splattered onto Sara's face.

Sara yelped and jumped up. Her companion got up too, cursing Hind in a dialect from somewhere on the eastern edge of the Arab world. Hind wiped tears of humiliation from her eyes and shouted at the man, "Aren't you ashamed to be sleeping with a married woman?" Sara grabbed Hind by the shoulder with one hand and planted a slap on her cheek with the other, then shouted, her eyes nearly popping out of her skull, "Shut up, you daughter of a whore!"

An uneasy silence fell over the café and seized Hind's tongue. She moved her lips but couldn't form any words. She pursed her lips, clenched her fists, and rose up on her tip toes. Everyone thought she was going to lunge at Sara's throat, but instead she spun around and ran for the bathroom, where she gave in to her tears. All she could think in that moment was how much she hated her boyfriend Aymen for leaving her, and how much she hated her brother Jawad.

No, not just hated him. She loathed him. He was the reason for all of this.

Her coworker went after her and tapped on the open door before coming inside. Hind turned to him. She furrowed her brow and glared at him, trying to frighten him. Then she grabbed his lapel and pulled him towards her. She pushed him up against the wall with her body, pressing her lips against his. He was so caught off guard that it took him a full minute to push Hind away. Then he ran out as though the devil himself were after him.

Hind looked at herself in the mirror. She took a deep breath, then let it out slowly. She straightened her blouse, fixed her hair, washed and dried her face. She checked her appearance again. She stood up straight, furrowed her brow and, with a frown fixed upon her face, went out to finish her shift.

CHAPTER 14

Brave New World

Days passed, followed by nights. Weeks turned into months until nearly three months had gone by since that summer day when Jawad was struck by the curse. It is afternoon now. The father is at the mosque. The mother has taken the bread dough to the neighborhood oven. The sister is cleaning the living room. Kneeling on the floor, her house dress tucked up around her thighs, she scrubs vigorously as she sings a soft French song in her gentle voice. Through all this, Jawad has been sleeping.

Once upon a time there was, or there wasn't, a kindhearted young man named Jawad who was struck by a curse that turned him into a creature whose presence no one could bear. He spent three months locked in his room, waking only for a few hours in the morning before surrendering to sleep once more for the rest of the day and all of the night. Or so he believed.

That afternoon, all the hair on his body stood on end, sensing a disturbance in the air's electricity. His sister's song made its way into his ears just as his nose picked up an unfamiliar masculine scent pervading the air. Jawad's eyes flew open and, acting on pure instinct, he jumped out of bed, burst through the door, and crashed straight into the French tourist, the one who was renting the spare room, just as he was about to straddle Hind from behind.

Hind screamed and so did the Frenchman, Emanuel, frightened by the monkey who had burst in on him.

The front door was flung open and in came the father, who had heard the scream from the stairwell, followed by his wife. He saw his daughter kneeling in one corner, and the young Frenchman in the other, screaming hysterically and pointing at Jawad, who was crouched on all fours as though about to pounce.

The father saw red. He demanded to know what was going on. The Frenchman kept pointing at Jawad and blathered a few words, from which the father understood that the monster had left his room and attacked the poor Frenchman, who had been carrying a bucket of water to help his honorable daughter with the cleaning. Jawad snarled but couldn't form a single word. The father turned first to the mother and let a few words of blame escape through his teeth for leaving their daughter alone in the house with a strange man. Then he turned to Hind to ask her. She remained silent for a moment as she looked back and forth from the Frenchman to her brother, then confirmed the Frenchman's story.

The Frenchman couldn't understand Hind's words, but understood from her gestures that she had corroborated his tale.

Jawad snarled again and looked like he was about to pounce on the Frenchman, but the father began beating him with the broomstick and pushing him back into his room, while trying to explain the inexplicable to the Frenchman and apologizing for the disturbance.

Little Amal giggled when Jawad passed by. His heart broke when he realized he hadn't played with her, or even gone near her, for three months. He reached his hand toward her on his way to his room, and his fingertips brushed her delicate hand. He froze for a moment before withdrawing his hand quickly, but it was too late. Dark images flowed from the child's fingertips into his consciousness like arrows in the army's burlap practice targets. His wife was showering and his father praying the afternoon prayer. His mother and sister had gone to the market. The wife stepped out of the shower wrapped only in a towel, forgetting or pretending to forget that she was not alone. The towel caught on the corner of the TV stand and slipped open. The father stood and folded up his prayer rug. His eyes were fixed on the houri that had descended to him from heaven. She hesitated for a moment, gasped, and ran out. His eyes followed the curve of her buttocks as she hurried out and his saliva caught in his throat. He coughed until he nearly choked. Then he rose, puffed up his chest, and strode towards her room. At first there was silent protest, then playful reluctance, then yielding acquiescence, and nine months later, there was Amal.

Jawad turned to his father, and his father could see in his son's eyes what he had seen. His shoulders slumped and his back drooped and he turned his gaze to the ground. Jawad returned to his room, and the foreigner to his, and the family sunk into a silence, which the mother broke with a fit of sobs followed by a prayer that Allah take her son's soul and relieve him and his family from their suffering. Hind followed her mother's prayer with an Amen. The father raised his eyes to look at them but remained in silent thought.

Jawad heard everything, and this time let the tears flow from his eyes. He remembered that Saturday morning, before the Monday of his metamorphosis, when he had gone to the medical testing lab to pick up the results that confirmed his suspicions. He was infertile and had no possibility whatsoever of fathering a child. He froze when he saw the results. He couldn't believe it. He slept peacefully that night, but the news awoke with him on Sunday morning and kept running through his veins like poison until he flung the results into the sewer by Malabatta Beach.

Jawad closed his eyes, never to open them again.

The mother and her daughter would awaken at dawn to the sound of the father reciting Surat Yasin in a trembling voice. The mother emerged from her room, hand over her heart, and the daughter emerged from hers and went straight to look in on the monster, but no one was there. They waited anxiously until the father finished his recitation and told them, before they had time to ask, that Jawad had passed away. He had already gotten rid of the monster's putrid, deformed corpse. The mother sat and sobbed silently and a smile passed fleetingly over the sister's face before she had time to hide it.

CHAPTER 15

The Days (3)

Tuesday, November 29th: Is he really dead? Could it be that his heart stopped from grief? Or, I wonder, did he kill himself on purpose? I wouldn't be surprised if our dear father dealt the final blow, after the scandal he caused with our French guest, and finished him off. But does it really matter? No. No. It does not.

Friday, December 2nd: Today I got my passport back with my Schengen visa inside. Emanuel set up a scholarship for me through one of his friends, at a yearlong artists' residency for Arab women writers, so I can write my first novel. But I'm not planning to come back. I'm going to put a final dot at the end of these lines, pick up my suitcase, and go far away from this miserable place. Emanuel, my love, is waiting for me at the port. Goodbye, Mama. Goodbye, Tangier.

Made in the USA
Las Vegas, NV
13 February 2023

67408596R00052